Y.U.K. Say!!
YOU UNBELIEVABLE KIDS

Y.u.K. Say!!
YOU UNBELIEVABLE KIDS

Jeanie Stanton

XULON PRESS

Xulon Press
2301 Lucien Way #415
Maitland, FL 32751
407.339.4217
www.xulonpress.com

Paperback ISBN-13: 978-1-6628-1983-4
Ebook ISBN-13: 978-1-6628-1984-1

ACKNOWLEDGMENTS

In memory of mom,
Because of you, I do what I do.

Excellent Illustrator Emily
Because you believe in me.

It's such a joy to have worked with you Roy.

And John, my brother, you're like no other.

Thanks so very much!

TABLE OF CONTENTS

INTRODUCTION

This fun filled fictional book of poetry is designed to help young readers, ages 9-11 to tap into their creative side and to voice their imagination through poetry as in the case of the Chameleon and The Praying Mantis. The Chameleon's overconfidence is short-lived, rather than catch a meal at his finger tip, a mouth-watering Mantis, he becomes a morsel instead. However, the Chameleon reappears on several occasions, thus, the Chameleon and the Praying Mantis, at some point, becomes the best of friends.

y.u.K. Say!! You Unbelievable Kids

I'll take you down a path of rhymes

Like mom did me plenty of times,

as I bounced upon her knees,

'Tell me again, pretty please?'

She'd look at me and say,

"What for?" I simply thought,

I gotta have more.

Enough said, so let's go!

I'M A POET

I'm a pretty good poet,

Most often show it.

I can think of a rhyme

On the spin of a dime,

For instance; mellow yellow,

Weird looking fellow,

Fat cat, stink in' rat,

Fish in the water.

Who thinks he's an Otter,

Comes easy to me as you can see

At the drop of a hat.

I'm a poet, I know it and that's that.

SHADOW ON THE WALL

Crying, coughing,sneezing, screaming,

My little brother keeps on dreaming;

Dreaming he has seen a monster,

I'd nod my head at the little youngster.

"The monster's big, black and furry,

Come! come!, Hurry, hurry".

'Where is that big, black and furry monster?

I don't see him, I don't see her'.

"There he is, big, black, furry and tall",

'Why that's not a monster at all,

It's your shadow on the wall'.

SOUND OF MUSIC

Music rings loudly in my ear,

The kind of noise I like to hear.

Drum, piano, violin,

Flute, toot, whistle, play it again.

The sound of music is in the air,

It seems to me it's everywhere,

In the valley, up the hill,

Through the woods I hear it still,

The sound of music, oh how sweet,

Musical notes are rather neat.

SMILE LIKE THE DOLPHINS

Dolphins have a lot of teeth,

That's one big fish that I won't eat,

To me it has a pretty smile,

I stare at it for a while.

Teeth on all their faces

Are so straight they need no braces.

I know someone who's name is Keith,

The dentist pulled out all his teeth.

I just want a pretty smile,

Like the dolphin that's my style.

PARTY BY INVITATION

I knocked on the door, nobody let me in.

I tapped on the windowpane over and
over again,

Rung the bell on the little door,

Right by the big house,

Then I rang the door once more.

Bicycles were parked on the lawn,

Where was everybody,

Including my friend Dawn?

Right around the house, in the very back,

Oddly, Dawn stared at me

Along with my friend Jack.

With one accord, they said,

"This party is by invitation only!

Let me guess, you feel pretty lonely".

OFF TO THE RODEO

Off to the rodeo,

I bought a ticket so I can go,

See cows and llamas, things like that,

Blue jeans , big boots and cowboy hats,

Pet short-legged dog,

Ride pony, dodge bull,

PAY $6 dollars to shave sheeps wool.

The taste of barbecue oh how dandy,

Mouth full of surgery cotten candy.

The smell of rodeo is in the air,

No doubt about it, I'll be there.

WHAT I WANT

What I want to be when I grow up is
an engineer,

Where I want to go when I am grown,

Is far away from here.

I think I'll go to Africa or to Italy,

I'll go from place to place and be all
that I can be.

I'll sail across the ocean on the deepsea blue,

I won't forget my BFF,

My best friend forever, is you.

IT'S ONLY HAIR

My hair is bushy still I'm happy,
Some people call it rough hair, even nappy.
Your hair is silky, shiny and long
Like Sally, my doll who sings a silly song.
Reggie's hair is rather curly,
He gets up for school pretty early.
Your hair is brown, mine is black,
Kat's a red-head just like Mac,

Speaking of hair on our head,
Of that subject there's much to be said.
Some kids have no hair at all,
My friend Perry has gone bald.

I love my nappy hair,

what others think I don't care.

I CAN COOK

I know that I can cook so,

Why did you give me that crummy old
cook book?

I can cook beans and things

Straight from my head as

Easy as pickle and lettuce placed on rye bread.

Maybe there is some things can't cook,

On second thought, I'll look in the book;

Wow! Spices like cumin, blackpepper and curry,

With this dish, I'll be in no hurry.

Thanks to the cookbook, my meal was yummy.

I've acted as if I was the biggest dummy.

The book makes cooking fun and easy,

Like Meatball-Pizza, nice and cheesy.

IT ITCHES IN MY BRITCHES

It itches in my britches. Oh my, how it hurts.

I probably got the itches from playing
in the durt

Or maybe it came from a dingy old cat,

While wrestling with Pete on the dingy
cat's mat.

I could have gotten it from the ants marching
out- door,

While sitting down near them on a
wooden floor.

I'm just about to figure out the reason

why, it itches in my britches.

A BIG FAT JUICY PICKLE

In my pocket there wasn't any,

No money there, not even a penny.

Surprised I was, to looked on the ground,

Two quarters, dime and some pennies I found.

The pennies equaled one nickel.

I've got just enough to buy me a big fat
juicy pickle.

LITTLE OLD LADY

There's a little old lady sitting in my house,

Reading book after book and as quiet
as a mouse.

I'll play loud music, sing and dance too,

'Just a little curious what will the little
old lady do?

Up! Up! Jumps the little old lady out of her
seat,   Going with the flow to the sound
of the beat.

MY NEW GLASSES

With my new glasses I can see

Creepy Crawlers climbing up a tree.

I can spot tiny particles on the ground,

As small as sugar my glasses found.

Only when I have them on, take them

off and small things are gone.

I really appreciate my new glasses,

More than momma's homemade surp, she

calls molasses.

JOHNNY, IN A BABY HIGHCHAIR

Can't get little Johnny out of his seat,

The nerves of him to ask for treats.

Ice cream, bubblegum and lollypop.

He whines for what he wants and will not stop,

Watches show after show in a baby highchair,

At five years old, he shouldn't be there.

Sometimes I feel like "nobody cares"!

I might as well live in a cave with the bears.

MY FAVORITE SPORT

Socker, hockey or baseball is my
favorite sport,

I'm not so sure of basketball 'cause I'm much
too short.

The hoop on the pole is way too high,

I'd get teased if I so much as give it a try.

Kids would say, "give it all you got,

Bet you can't make that shot".

Give me, hockey my team would win,

With my eyes on the puck, it'll go right in.

GUESS HOW MANY

In my family there are plenty,

Boys and girls, guess how many?

Count ten fingers and then toes,

There's more in my family so on you go.

Count head to head, it sounds like fun,

Count all over again, you'd probably miss one.

Try living in a house with that many,

Ask for; "seconds please"! There aren't any.

AN AFGHAN

I've got an Afghan.

It's not a blanket or shawl,

Funny how thing are the same

Yet not the same at all.

I've got an Afghan, a strange, long-nose looking dog.

I take him to the park with me,

When I go out to jog.

CHICKEN SOUP

I got the sniffles,

I am about to sneeze,

Move far away from me, if you please!

It's those wiggly gilly things called worms,

I'm simply sick of nasty germs.

I've seen them under the microscope,

But there's hope when hands are washed
with soap.

I need just one humongous scoop,

Of grandpa's Get-Well Chicken Soup.

CLOUDY OUTSIDE

It's cloudy outside and thundering,

Boom! Boom! The storm has got me
wondering,

Why is thunder followed by lightning?

The sound of it is quite frightening.

A Rain-Massague could be such fun

Dark clouds instead make me run.

For now, I'll stay indoors,

Complete my homework and finish my chores.

RAINBOW IN THE SKY

There's

A rainbow in the sky,

With seven colors, I wonder why

It is red, yellow, orange, green and blue,

Also violet and indigo too?

I can imagine it's colors are

Red and white, of peppermint candy

And I take a big bite, then slide the slope
of the arch all the way down, from the sun
straight to the grown.

FEEL THE WIND BLOW

I can feel the wind blow against my skin,

I can see leaves dancing in trees every
now and then.

Summertime pollen tickles my nose and makes
me sneeze,

Windy weather of wintertime makes
me freeze.

I can feel the wind blow,

But where does it go? I really don't know.

BLUE JEANS

I've got a pair of blue jeans,

I never thought I'd get,

I tried them on, but I won't wear them yet.

I'll fold them rather neatly and put them in
the dresser drawer,

I wonder, who bought them for me?

From what store, and so much more?

I like to wear blue jeans a lot, whether it's
cold outside or not.

BUMBLE BEE

I was stung by a bumble bee,

My oh my, how it hurt when he stung me.

but he must not have done it on purpose,

'Cause, in a jar the bee left all of us,

A sweet treat of golden yellow honey,

Suddenly, the sting was the thing that
was funny,

Now we've got lots of honey for no money.

PEANUT BUTTER SANDWICH

Peanut Butter sandwich is what I love to eat.

The nutty buttery taste of it

Makes a dandy treat.

It wood get messy if I chew,

Here's what happens when I do,

Stuff comes oozing out my mouth,

It goes north and then goes south,

I'll mind my manners and chew with style,

That is all it takes to grin and smile.

WE RISE

Up early in the morning to do my thing,

Suddenly the doorbell begins to ring,

On my way and ready to go

With my friends to make our third trek

In the snow.

We go to the mountain, head straight
for the Top,

First and second time,

Was a big flop.

Mountain climbing was indeed an eyeopener,

It wasn't easy for me, him or her.

Finally, we've reached the top,

Oh what a surprise!

Not bad for someone of our size.

For once, we rise!

CHAMELEON AND THE PRAYING MANTIS

There once was a hungry Chameleon

Who admired himself,

He would change colors from one to another

While standing by a mirror next to

A wooden shelf.

Protected, so he thought, from snakes

And birds. The Chameleon
considered nothing of

Large animals that pack in herds.

Along came a Mantis to pray upon the
Chameleon's Cheek, "Hum", he started sob-
bing, "will her prayer

Last as long as a week"?

The Chameleon continued, "I will ask
the Mantis

To teach me how to pray.

She will know what things I ought to say".

However, the Mantis looked at him and

Swiftly flew away.

The chameleon let out a sigh as the
Praying Mantis flew by,

"Have I missed my meal on this very day?"

As for the Chameleon, there was

nothing more to say.

A slithery snake looked his way,

Then said, "No time to lose", and he

Immediately gulped down his multi
colored prey.

Meanwhile the Praying Mantis had enjoyed

Her getaway to a faraway City in Atlantis.

While in Atlantis and basking in the
summer sun,

The Praying Mantis, with time on hand,

she had lots of fun.

All of a sudden, the Mantis replied,

"As she look up with beaming eyes ,then said,

this is quite an eerie surprise."

'Why should it be a surprise to you?

In the field, I do what I do,

I look high and low, in and out,

Changing my colors as I move about'.

The Chameleon replied coolly.

At that moment, the Praying Mantis pre-
tended to be

A friend, of the Chameleon;

She doesn't want to be met with her end.

The Praying Mantis whispered, "I must
fly away",

Although uncertain, she was invited to stay.

The Chameleon had all but good intention.

No doubt, he failed to mention,

Who was the predator and who was the prey,

He simply looked the other way.

Meanwhile, the Praying Mantis had no

Time to lose. She made her getaway

On the six o'clock cruise.

There at the pier was a huge rock, a

Resting place fit for a Queen,

The Mantis had no clue that the Chameleon

Would be there, she said, "Who would have
Thought such a thing".

She went on to say, "How did you get here, what time did you arrive, are you really alive?"

The Chameleon replied, "You must have me confused with one of my brothers. One is no more but I have many others." He continued,

"Now quietly come with me to dinner,

I'll have you for supper, I am a winner".

The Mantis wasted no time to think,

Right by her side was a feather and ink.

She thought for a moment, "If only I

Could write a letter and pray that things

Would get better". Swiftly, the Chameleon excused himself, to look in the mirror by a

Wooden shelf. Now, with no time to waste,

The Mantis Began to write since the
Chameleon was clear out of sight.

"Family and friends, I'll

Miss you a lot, mostly you, Dot and Scott".

The Chameleon insisted on having his way,
He went off to plan what to do and prepare
what to say.

In an instant, the Chameleon was back.

Oddly, He arrived with a friend of the Mantis,

Who had worn a backpack.

The Chameleon exclaimed, "What's good for
the goose is good for the gander, meet my
good Friend Salamander".

It was as if the Chameleon tipped his hat

And that was that.

In a strange sort of way came the end
of the day

With an unusual celebration, all had become
the best of friends and parted ways at

Fifth Street Train Station.

Now safe and sound in her own habitat,

The Mantis couldn't wait to talk

About this and that, pertaining to what

Happened on that day,

About how things could have turned out

In a very different way.

The Mantis' friend with the backpack,

Held the key that set her free.

Out of his backpack came slugs and bugs,

What seemed like a gazillion, to satisfy

The appetite of the hungry Chameleon.

"Time flies", said the Praying Mantis as
she gathered her thoughts.

She continued, back to the Chameleon I will go,

Only for a short while, to say a brief hello".

The Praying Mantis was steered with excite-
ment, "I won't

Forget to bring a backpack, just incase

His stomach is empty, i'll

leave him absolutely no reason to eat me".

As if by magic, the Chameleon appeared

With much enthusiasm,

Instantly, the Mantis went into a spasm.

The Chameleon jeered,

"Don't bother to come to me, I've come

To you. Haven't I told you that I do what I do?

I look high and low, in and out,

Changing my colors as I move about".

The Mantis considered that things could get

Rather sticky, as a friend of the
Chameleon who was ever so tricky.

She screamed, "I was completely startled"!

"Nothing goes wrong when you do as you're
told", replied the Chameleon.

The Mantis said softly, "I thought we were
friends, you said so, where has our friendship
gone, tell me if you know?"

The Chameleon chuckled, "Yuk, yuk, yuk", 'Do
As You're Told',

"Is the name of a song, your welcome,

My dear, to sing along.

Sit down, sit down, sit down.

Turn your frown around!"

After that the jokes got started. They

Laugh more than a little bit,

And just wouldn't quit.

Both were up until the break of dawn,

Finally the Mantis let out a big yawn,

Then said, "I'm Mara, the Mantis and

What is your name?"

'Cameron, the camouflage Chameleon.

I live outdoors, and do what I do as

I told you before'.

The Mantis bravely kept the conversa-
tion going.

Among other things, she talked about

how green

The grass had been growing.

The Mantis went on to discuss,

Matters pertaining to her family,

For whom she had a longing.

"It's a lovely evening, wouldn't you agree?"

Presume the Mantis.

The Chameleon replied, "Yes, day or night, the
time is right, it's all the same to me".

Immediately he changed the subject.
"I know of

A game called hide and seek".

Mara the Mantis wasted no time to speak,

"It's been a long day, perhaps I'll see you

Again, say, in about a week?"

Cameron the Chameleon thanked her for her

hospilatily and went away.

Mara the Mantis was unsure that he'd be

Gone forever or come back

on the very next day.

Just in case he would return, Mara considered

What she might say to him,

She would ask about

His family, and how she wants

To know all about them.

The Mantis refused to let the Chameleon

See her quiver and shiver,

Surely not Find her hide

underneath the rug.

Mara the Mantis, quickly thought of a solution,

"Hum"! She said,

"I'll kindly invite Cameron the
Camouflage Chameleon

To dinner, and serve on a platter his

Favorite finger foods,

A gazillion slugs and bugs".

A BALL CAN BOUNCE UP AND DOWN

POEMS CAN CIRCLE THE WORLD AROUND

Now that it's all said and done,

I hope you, like me,

had lots' of fun.

THE END

CPSIA information can be obtained
at www.ICGtesting.com
Printed in the USA
LVHW070446201021
700838LV00009B/165

9 781662 819834